D1494424

DREAMWORKS
Spirit
RIDING FREE

LUCKY'S DIARY

EGMONT

We bring stories to life

First published in 2018 in North America / United States by Little,
Brown and Company. This edition published in Great Britain in 2020
by Egmont UK Limited
2 Minster Court, 10th floor, London EC3R 7BB
www.egmont.co.uk

ISBN 978 1 4052 99176
71168/001
Printed in the United Kingdom

Cover Design by Ching Chan

Egmont takes its responsibility to the planet
and its inhabitants very seriously. We aim to use papers from well-
managed forests run by responsible suppliers.

Lucky's Diary

STACIA DEUTSCH

Diary Entry

Today was the worst best day ever.

First, the best part. School is out for the summer! I mean, what's better than that? Nothing that I can think of. Nothing! And <u>nothing</u> is the whole point of summer. Not a thing. No school books. No packed lunches. No homework. Nowhere to be when the rooster crows. Nothing. Doesn't that sound wonderful?

Doing nothing was my perfect summer holiday plan until the best day turned into the worst.

This is <u>exactly</u> what happened:

After shouting, 'Meet you at the barn!' I left my friends in front of school. Spirit was already waiting for me by the old oak tree.

I wrapped my arms tightly around my wild stallion's neck and gave him a big smooch on the smooth caramel-coloured hair just above his warm black nose. He snorted at me, so I kissed him again, when I really knew he wanted the apple in my bag.

'I'm just teasing you,' I told him, and gave up the red delicious treat. Spirit gobbled it in one big bite, and we were off.

We took a quick stop home to drop off my schoolbag. Adiós, books and pencils and notebooks! See ya next year.

Abigail had this big idea to start the Summer of Spirit (which she is calling Summer of Boomerang) with a horse spa day. Pru loved that idea and thought her horse, Chica Linda, could use some grooming. For Pru's last birthday, her dad gave her this amazing grooming kit. It had a curry brush, two soft brushes, a hoof pick, and special mane and tail brushes in a beautiful carved wooden box. Pru wanted us all to share the first time she used it, so she saved it for today!

Abigail had used her allowance to buy some rainbow-coloured ribbons for her horse, Boomerang, but she could never decide which colour matched Boomerang's tail the best, so she decided to wait to use them until today, too. There were plenty for all our horses. Even Spirit, if he wanted ribbons.

I was the only one who didn't have something special to contribute to spa day, and I really wanted to share something, too. So after I shoved my bag into a corner by the door, I started looking around the house.

I could take more apples for a snack. But that didn't seem very special.

With a final glance around the kitchen, I shouted out to Spirit through the window, 'Be right back!' and went upstairs. There had to be something good that we all could use.

Fluffy towels for drying off after the horses' wash? My dad might not like it when I brought back soggy towels covered in horse hair.

In my desk drawer, I had a mud mask that Abigail's brother, Snips, gave me for Christmas. It looked like black gunk in a jar. I'd never opened it, so I thought maybe it would be a good addition to spa day. We could do mud masks for the horses! I unscrewed the lid. <u>Ack</u>! It smelled horrible. When I looked closer at the glass container, I could see bits of rotten food stuck in the mud. He had obviously filled the jar with mud from the pig pen! <u>Yuck</u>. I sealed the lid and dropped the whole thing in the trash.

I'd never make Spirit do a stinky mud mask on spa day. Besides, he was already covered in mud from his night with the herd. (I sometimes wonder what they do when they are together.) Seriously, Spirit could use a walk through the river, or maybe a bath ...

Oh, that gave me an idea.

Aunt Cora had moved out of the house and into the inn, but there were a few of her things left in a box downstairs. I knew exactly what I needed.

Skipping two stairs at a time, I returned to the kitchen. In the back of the pantry was Cora's box. I bet she'd even forgotten about it. I dragged the box into the light and dug down deep. There were a couple of frilly aprons, a pair of silver candlesticks, a photo of her and my dad when they were young, and there … at the bottom … was a crystal bottle filled with a light-purple liquid.

I held up the bottle towards the window. The crystal glittered in the afternoon sunlight, casting rainbows on the kitchen walls. It was the prettiest bottle I'd ever seen. For as long as I could recall, I'd seen it on her dressing table by her hairbrush and hand mirror. I knew when it was empty, Aunt Cora could refill the beautiful bottle at the supermarket in town.

I looked and now the bottle was full to the top. I slowly pulled out the stopper, careful not to spill even a drop of the precious purple liquid inside. Raising the bottle to my nose, I took a deep breath.

The most amazing scent filled the room: lavender flowers with a hint of lemon.

I held the bottle towards the window and let the crystal cast more dancing rainbows on the ceiling and floor.

'Hey, Spirit,' I called out to where he stood, waiting for me in the shady spot of the yard. 'How would you like a bubble bath?'

Spirit whinnied.

'Sounds great, right?'

I knew this was the perfect thing I could to add to the PALs' Horse Spa Day. We could wash Chica Linda, Boomerang and Spirit with Aunt Cora's bubble bath. Groom them with Pru's brushes. Then, tie Abigail's ribbons in their manes and tails.

When I jumped on Spirit's back to ride over to the barn, I smiled. The Summer of Spirit was off to the perfect start.

And then everything went totally <u>wrong</u>.

Turned out that Boomerang didn't like the smell of the lavender-scented bubble bath. When Abigail put a little of the purple soap in her hand, he backed away from her.

'Try it again,' I encouraged as I poured some into my hand, then passed the bottle to Pru.

I reached up to slather Spirit. He caught one whiff of the lavender and protested loudly as well, huffing and moving back away from my hand.

'Oh, come on, Spirit,' I cooed. 'You'll smell like Aunt Cora.'

I guess Spirit wasn't into smelling like Aunt Cora.

Abigail was still struggling to put the soap on Boomerang. She was chasing him in and out of barn stalls with her hand held high.

'Maybe the horses would have liked the smell of Snips's stinky mud better?' she suggested. Abigail admitted she'd tried the mud mask. She said it made her eyes water for a week. No matter how much she scrubbed, she couldn't get the smell off!

I remembered that after Christmas, she'd worn a garlic necklace around her neck. She told me and Pru it was to keep away vampires in the new year. I should have guessed it was because garlic smelled better than the mud!

So, here's how the day went from good to bad to worse:

Chica Linda was the only one willing to take a bubble bath. She got all

soapy and slippery. She was loving it,
but then, just as Pru was handing me
back the crystal bottle, Boomerang
reared up, once again backing away
from Abigail.

Pru's hands were slippery from
the bubbles. Since Spirit wouldn't
let me put soap on him, my hands
still had the soap dollop I'd intended
to use. That meant my hands were
slippery, too.

When Boomerang bumped Abigail,
she bumped Spirit. Spirit bumped
me and I dropped the crystal bubble
bath bottle. The good news was that
before it crashed down, I reached
out and caught it again by throwing
myself over a barrel of oats with an
outstretched hand.

But just as I was about to celebrate, I heard the distinct clatter of crystal on the barn floor.

<u>What was that?</u> I wondered.

It was the lid. I hadn't caught the bottle <u>and</u> the stopper. Just the bottle.

Abigail shouted when she saw the diamond-shaped stopper on the floor near me. It was casting rainbows of light on the barn walls, which was pretty, but made it hard to see exactly where the stopper was ... We searched through wet bubbles and around horses until ...

<u>CRACK.</u>

Boomerang stepped on it.

It wasn't Boomerang's fault, or Spirit's for bumping me. Or Pru's for having slippery hands. Or even Chica

Linda's fault. She had been the one who loved the bath.

Later, when I went to see Aunt Cora, I had to explain that the broken crystal stopper was all my fault. The truth was hard, but I told it. I'd taken the bubble bath from her box. I'd brought the crystal bottle to the barn.

Aunt Cora was pretty nice about it all. She didn't yell at me. Or ground me for life, which is what I expected. She didn't even tell my father. She sat calmly on her sofa, looking at the empty bottle and the broken stopper.

And then she said the words that ruined my summer holiday.

'Lucky,' Aunt Cora told me, 'you will need to earn money this summer to replace the bottle and fill it with bubble bath.' She looked me straight in the eye. 'I like lavender.'

The Summer of Spirit was over before it had even started. I won't be doing nothing all summer after all. The best day turned into the worst because ...

I need a job.

CHAPTER 1

'Mr Winthrop!'
The instant the ice cream shop
opened, Lucky flew through the door. 'Mr
Winthrop!' she called again. When he didn't
reply, her first instinct was to check behind
the counter. That's where she'd found him
that time his back went out.

He wasn't there. She called again. 'Mr
Winthrop! Where are you?'

Lucky looked around the shop. There
was a long counter for ice cream and some
tables with chairs. She'd worked there for a
few weeks while Mr Winthrop's back healed.
It was after Spirit got hurt and he was
healing, too. Lucky had liked working there

15

and hoped he might need some help for the summer.

'Hello, Lucky.' Mr Winthrop stuck his head out from the back room. He was wearing his work apron. 'How can I help you this fine day? I was just whipping up some new butter pecan. Would you like some?'

'Oh, I'm not here for ice cream,' Lucky said, though butter pecan sounded delicious. 'I was hoping for a summer position.' She rolled up on her tiptoes to look older and more mature since the last time she'd worked there.

'Ah,' Mr Winthrop said, studying Lucky closely. 'Yes, you were very helpful.'

Lucky smiled. 'I know! Who would have guessed it was so difficult to serve ice cream?' In fact, she'd given the customers some confusing advice along with their cones, but it all turned out okay in the end. 'I'd like to take another try at the job, if I can.'

'I'm sorry, Lucky,' Mr Winthrop told her. 'We just can't afford a worker this summer.'

'But who will give advice with the cones?' Lucky lamented.

'I suppose,' Mr Winthrop said with a thoughtful smile, 'that will have to be me.'

'Are you sure?' Lucky asked, getting desperate. 'What about at your supermarket? Do you need help there?'

'Same answer, Lucky,' answered Mr Winthrop.

Lucky felt her frustration rising. 'Are you absolutely sure I can't have a job? I really need one, and I already asked at the bank and the library.' Ice cream scooping had been Lucky's first choice, but when she'd arrived in town, the shop was closed. She'd gone around town asking other places while waiting for it to open.

'Sorry,' Mr Winthrop told her. 'Perhaps you can come up with a unique idea, something the town needs but no one has thought of yet ...' He returned to the back room.

Feeling sad and uncertain about what to do next, Lucky left the shop.

Spirit was waiting in the square.

'What am I going to do?' she asked him, putting a hand on his nose and giving him a soft scratch. Spirit dipped to make it easier for her to climb on, but she didn't want to ride yet. They walked a bit together. 'I'm out of ideas,' she groaned.

Moving slowly down the sidewalk, Lucky dragged her feet while Spirit tried to lift her mood by nudging her playfully. When they reached the supermarket, Lucky stopped. A crystal bottle in the window caught Lucky's eye. She was drawn to it, watching the way the cut glass sparkled. It was not exactly like

18

the one she'd broken, but it was very close. It wasn't as if Lucky could buy only a new stopper for Cora's bottle; she had to buy the whole thing. And she was certain that Aunt Cora would like this one very much. She went inside, raised the glass, and looked at the tag. It was so expensive … and she knew it would cost even more to refill the bubble bath.

She sighed and asked Spirit, 'How will I ever earn enough money? It's hopeless! No one will hire me!'

At that, Spirit neighed and Lucky followed the way he was gazing. In the distance, she could see a puff of smoke from a passing train.

'You think I should ask my dad?' Lucky stopped walking to watch the black puff of smoke dissipate into the blue sky. 'He isn't going to want me working the trains or pounding rail spikes.' She considered it.

'Perhaps I could sell tickets or drinks at the station?' That was a good idea.

Spirit whinnied.

'Thanks, Spirit.' She put a hand up and rubbed his back. 'If Dad says yes, I'll get you an extra apple.'

Spirit whinnied again.

'Ten apples,' she corrected, and climbed onto his back for the short ride home.

'Agggh,' Lucky complained to her friends when they went for an afternoon ride. 'Dad said he didn't have any jobs at the railroad. Seriously, that was my last, last, last idea. I need to buy Cora a new bottle, but I don't know how.' She squeezed her legs around Spirit a bit tighter. The horse responded by quickening his pace to keep up with the others.

'You can help me babysit Snips,' Abigail suggested, keeping her eyes on the horizon as Boomerang sped across the green valley. 'Maybe if two of us watched him together, he'd act like a normal kid.'

Pru laughed as Chica Linda pulled up next to Spirit. 'Wishful thinking,' she said. 'Your little brother doesn't even know what *normal* means.'

Abigail scratched her head. 'What if he was the normal one, and we were all weird?'

Pru laughed even harder, and Lucky joined in, chuckling.

'It's true. He's a strange little brother,' Abigail said. She glanced at Lucky. 'But you can still help me babysit.'

Lucky considered it for a moment. 'What does babysitting Snips pay?'

'Oh, I should have told you that,' Abigail said with a frown. 'Nothing. It's more like a chore than a job. I guess that's not very helpful, huh?'

'*Nothing* won't buy a new glass bottle at the shop.' Lucky sighed. 'Thanks anyway.' With that idea out, she turned to Pru. 'What are you doing this summer?' Then she quickly added, 'And can I help?'

'Not unless you want to go to Rancho El Paseo,' Pru said. 'My dad is sending me there for the summer to help his cousin Raymond with his new ranch.'

Lucky gasped. 'You're not going to be here all summer?'

'But that's too long,' Abigail moaned. 'You can't go away all summer! What will we do without you? Don't go, Pru.' She pouted. 'You have to stay in Miradero. It will be a terrible summer if we aren't all together.'

'I know!' Pru lamented. 'That's what I told my dad, but he just said, 'You can't sit around all day.'

Lucky wrinkled her nose and groaned.

'Looks as if we'll all be busy this summer.' She slowed Spirit down near a small grove of trees and climbed from his back. Spirit immediately began to eat the grass. Pru and Abigail dismounted as well, and Boomerang and Chica Linda wandered off to be with Spirit.

Abigail flopped back in the grass, staring up at the sky. 'It makes me sad that we can't spend our summer with the horses. The PALs, out riding the range, searching for adventure.' PAL was a combination of the three girls' names: Pru, Abigail, and Lucky.

Abigail watched the clouds roll by. 'That one looks like a little girl,' she said, pointing to a thick cloud with a puffy top. 'She's wearing a fancy hat.'

'I don't see a girl,' Pru said, lying back next to Abigail and squinting into the afternoon light. 'Sort of looks like a boy to me. He's got a big head, not a hat.'

'Oh, that's the one next to the girl,' Abigail said. 'Now it looks like the boy is chasing the girl. They're playing cloud tag.'

Lucky joined them on the grass.

'I still don't see it,' Pru said.

'They're having so much fun,' Abigail said, pointing. The clouds had shifted, and the two fluffy children were floating in different directions. 'They're getting ready to play a new game!' she exclaimed.

Lucky and Pru exchanged a baffled look. Neither of them saw what Abigail saw.

'It's like Red Rover,' Abigail told them. 'Only it's Prancing Ponies. Do you see the other cloud kids galloping like horses? It's so fun, everyone wants to join in!'

'That's it!' Lucky suddenly sat up and pointed at the clouds. 'We can make a day club!'

'For cloud children?' Abigail asked, staring at her. 'Why do fluffy cloud children need a club?'

'Not cloud children,' Pru said, also sitting up as she caught on. 'For-real children. The kids of Miradero!'

'Oh,' Abigail said. 'You're right, cloud kids don't need a club. They can just have fun playing games in the sky.'

'Exactly,' Lucky said with a giggle. 'But Miradero children would love as. Parents could send the kids to us and we could take care of them all day. We could play games—'

'Like Prancing Ponies!' Abigail put in.

'Yes!' Pru said.

'This is the best idea ever!' Abigail cheered. 'I'll get my mum and dad to sign up Snips! He'll be our first kid.'

'As long as he pays,' Lucky said. 'PALs Adventure Club can't be free.' She started to figure out the details. 'We can charge one pound for each child for the whole summer. Then, we can split up everything we make three ways. By the end of summer, I'll have plenty of money to buy a bottle, bottle top, and bubble bath for Aunt Cora, and I bet I can even afford something extra to decorate the barn. Do you think Spirit would like a pinwheel above his stall?'

'I know what I'll do with my earnings: I'm going to buy more ribbons,' Abigail said. 'Boomerang wants a new set of rainbow ones. Last night, Señor Carrots ate the orange ones from the package.' Señor Carrots was Snips's donkey.

'I hope he's okay,' Pru said. 'Donkeys shouldn't eat ribbons.'

'He burped them back up later,' Abigail said, then squished up her face and said, *'Eww.'*

'Boomerang deserves new ribbons,' Lucky agreed. She turned to Pru. 'What are you going to do with the money we earn at the club?'

'I'm going to – wait …' Pru paused, then looked down. She began to pick at the grass.

'What's wrong?' Lucky asked her.

'I'm committed to Rancho El Paseo,' she said. 'I can't help with the club.'

'I think we should ask your dad,' Lucky said. 'Maybe if we tell him all about our plans, he'd agree to let you stay. PALs Club wouldn't be nearly as much fun without you.'

'It won't be the PALs Club if we're not all here! If it's just Lucky and Abigail, it would be … the LA club. That doesn't even make any sense!'

Pru stood to get Chica Linda. 'Come on. Let's go ask him right now!' She climbed up, ready for the ride back to town.

Spirit came for Lucky. She pulled herself onto his back and wrapped her arms around his neck. 'We're going to make a club!' she told Spirit.

Spirit raised his head and broke into a trot.

'Wahoo!' Abigail shouted, as the PALs began the ride back to Miradero. 'Race you home!'

The three horses sped across the valley, back towards town.

The best summer ever was back on track.

Diary Entry

He said <u>YES</u>! Pru's dad said <u>YES</u>! I can hardly believe it.

We are going to have a summer club for the kids of Miradero! I'd sing a happy song, if I could, but I'll leave the singing at the club to Pru because she's great at it. Abigail is going to bring her best talent and teach the kids to bake. She'll start with her grandma's cherry pies. Grandma Stone's pies are so yummy that they win all the baking contests in town. Then, there's me. Since I am the only one who's had a paying job before,

I'll be in charge of the money and the business stuff.

There are so many things to do to have a successful club, and the first thing is to get kids signed up. The more kids we have, the more money we'll make.

After Pru got the good news, we talked about what our flyers should say. I agreed to make them at home.

We're meeting in a little while to post them around town.

I'm not a great artist, so I had Spirit help decorate the flyers. I spread them on the ground and explained. I had to stomp around to show Spirit what I wanted and he totally got it. We dipped his hooves in black paint, and he walked all over the pages. When the paint dried, the flyers looked great!

The flyers look like this:

PALs Adventure Club

Miradero Music
Tasty Treats
Glorious Games
Storytelling and Scavenger Hunts

All kids welcome. Only one pound.

Sign up this week with
your favourite counsellors:

Pru Granger, Abigail Stone, and
Lucky Prescott at the table in front
of the supermarket.

Here's the rest of the to-do list:

☑ Clipboard, paper and pencil to sign everyone up.

☑ Sign for the table.

☑ Pins to put up the flyers.

☑ A money box.

Check. Check. Check. Check. Yep. We've got it all.
Time to meet the kids.
I can't wait!

CHAPTER 2

'Put the last one on this tree.' Pru handed Lucky a flyer.

Reaching down, Lucky grabbed the paper. She was standing on Spirit's back to get high enough to post it.

Abigail handed Lucky a couple of pins, saying, 'Don't poke yourself. Believe me' – she held up her fingers, which all had little red prick marks, and sighed – 'it's not fun.'

'Thanks for the warning,' Lucky told Abigail. Spirit stood still while she pressed a pin through the poster, attaching it to a tree.

'*Hee-haw!*' Señor Carrots suddenly brayed. Since Snips was the first enrolled kid, Abigail had him pulling the donkey around town, helping advertise. Señor Carrots was wearing a double sign over his back that hung over each side. It said *PALs Adventure Club* on one sign and *We promise summer fun* on the other.

'I don't think you should promise we'll have fun,' Snips called out to Lucky. 'Señor Carrots and I have very high standards.' He sniffled and wiped his nose on his shirt. 'You shouldn't make promises you can't keep.'

'We *promise* the club will be fun,' Lucky assured him. She jumped down from Spirit's back, put away the pins, and moved over to a table in the street. Pru had borrowed the small table from her dad, along with three chairs for them to sit at it.

'I agree with Snips,' a low voice said, coming from behind Lucky. 'You shouldn't promise fun.'

Lucky hadn't leaned back yet in her chair

when she popped upright again. She knew that voice … but there was no way. Her cousin was at boarding school, wasn't he?

'Hello, RF,' Julian greeted with a low bow.

'Julian?' Lucky greeted, sounding a little confused. 'What are you doing here?!' It wasn't the nicest greeting, but she was surprised to see him.

'Nice to see you, too,' Julian said with a laugh. 'Don't worry, RF. I'm just here to visit Aunt Cora. I'm planning a great summer. Don't you want to have a great summer, too, like me?'

Lucky liked her cousin well enough, but he was so tricky. She reminded herself to tread cautiously where Julian was concerned. Whenever he came to town, he'd cause a big mess. He was a true-born con man – or rather, con *boy* as the PALs liked to say. She still wasn't completely over the first time he'd

35

visited Miradero and conned all the local kids into giving him their money to build a super-fast roller coaster ... which just turned out to be a regular old mine cart.

Still, family was family, and Lucky knew she should give him a chance. She wrapped her arm around him in a cautious hug. 'That's true. It'll be nice to have you here ... maybe.'

'That's better,' he said, gently pushing her back and greeting her friends. 'Nice to see Lucky's marvellous friends, too.'

Pru and Abigail were a lot more welcoming. Especially Abigail, who didn't always have the same suspicions about Julian's motives.

'Speaking of great summers, it looks as if things are busy here in Miradero. Whatcha up to?' Julian asked, looking at the table. 'What's this *fun* club all about, RF?'

Lucky exhaled sharply. She'd asked him

a million times not to call her *RF*. Julian
thought it was funny. Rabbits' feet were
supposed to be lucky, so he made that her
nickname. *Ugh*.

'We ...' she began slowly.

'We're having a summer club for the kids
of Miradero,' Abigail blurted out, and before
Pru or Lucky could stop her, she added,
'Lucky needs to earn some money to buy a
crystal bottle for—'

Lucky grabbed Abigail's arm and tugged
her back. She and Pru led her a few steps
away from Julian. 'Don't tell him so much,'
Lucky cautioned. 'He's still a con boy!'

'Got it,' Abigail said, and sauntered back
towards Julian. She whistled while her hands
swung casually by her side.

'So, you were explaining, Abigail, why does
Lucky need the money?' Julian asked when
the girls got back by the table.

''Cause she' – Abigail paused, looking over at Pru and Lucky – 'needs it.'

'You said she wanted to buy something,' Julian asked. 'What?'

'Don't we all want to buy things?' Abigail responded. 'Shoes, coats, hats, horse blankets, crystal bott—' She stopped herself again, then asked, 'What do *you* want to buy, Julian?' Abigail tipped her ear to listen.

'I'm not shopping,' Julian answered. 'And yet, like you, I need to make some money this summer. When I got permission to come to Miradero for the summer, I had to promise my mother that I'd get a job. If I don't find a job, she'll make me come back home and work at our neighbour's insurance office.' To show what he thought of that job, he yawned.

'Sounds as if you'll be an insurance man, then.' Lucky snorted. 'I've asked everyone in town. No one is hiring.'

'I heard about that,' Julian said, leaving Lucky to wonder if Aunt Cora had told him her woes. 'I'm not going to break my promise to my mum. I have a plan.' He picked up the PALs' club sign-up form and began reading the names and addresses of their new kids, before Lucky swooped it right out of his hands. Smiling at Lucky's dramatic dive for the sign-up sheet, Julian said, 'I believe I have something that can help you with your club. I saw you only have seven kids.'

'Well, six, actually,' Abigail corrected. 'We have Snips, Bianca, and her twin sister, Mary Pat. And then we have some new kids in town whose parents work for the railroad: Lilly and Lester. And then there's Maricela's little cousin, Stella.'

'And Turo is coming to help!' added Pru, before giving Lucky a bashful glance. Turo was too old to be at a club but he wanted to help out his friends, so he signed up.

Now, including the information that Turo wasn't paying, Julian did the maths. 'It would be better if you didn't have to split your earnings, because once you divide the money… you each won't earn very much, will you?'

This wasn't news. Lucky was aware that they needed at least two more kids if she wanted to get the bottle for Aunt Cora, fill it, and have a little money left over. She didn't reveal that, but Abigail did.

'We need to raise two more pounds,' she said. Then, realising she was once again oversharing with Julian, she put a hand over her own mouth and muttered, 'Darn it.'

'I see …' Julian said, glancing over his shoulder towards the ice cream shop. 'Do you want help from your old cousin Julian?'

At first, Lucky thought he wanted to be a

counsellor, too, but he assured them he felt that Lucky, Pru, and Abigail would be *much* better counsellors than he ever could be. 'Plus, I wouldn't want to ask you all to split your profits!' Julian added. 'No, no ... I'll find my own job for the summer ...'

Lucky wanted to know what Julian was up to. 'Then what do you have in mind?' she asked, slowly eyeing him for any funny stuff behind his answer.

'Two pounds,' he said, tapping his pants pocket as if he already had money there. 'I'll pay the price for two kids and all you need to do is take one.'

Just then, the door to the ice cream shop opened ...

'Be quick,' Julian said, glancing behind him. Lucky thought he might even be a bit nervous. 'You have to decide right now. Yes or no?'

'Whatever it is, we'll do it!' Abigail stepped between Pru and Lucky before either of them could ask any more questions or turn the deal down. At their look, she said, 'It's *two pounds*! All our problems will be solved.'

Pru gave in as well. 'And for just one kid.'

Lucky didn't understand why someone would pay *more* than the normal cost of the club, but her friends had already agreed. 'Who's the kid?' she asked Julian.

Aunt Cora stepped into the sunlight. Behind her was a young boy. He had an ice cream cone in one hand while Aunt Cora balanced two more cones.

'Here's your ice cream, Julian,' she said, handing the cone to him. 'Oh,' she said, seeing Lucky and her friends for the first time. 'Would you young ladies like some ice cream, too?'

'Sure,' Abigail said, answering for all of them. 'Thanks, Miss Prescott.'

'Happy to do it. I'm having a wonderful day now that Julian and Oliver are here,' she gushed. 'I didn't tell anyone they were coming. I wanted it to be a lovely surprise. I haven't even told your father yet,' she told Lucky.

Aunt Cora was very proud that she'd kept this a big secret. 'Oliver, stay here and get to know your cousin.' She stepped back, humming happily. 'Ice cream for everyone. I'll be right back,' she said, quickening her steps towards the shop.

'Oliver?' Lucky said, looking at the boy. He had short brown hair that he swept to the side like Julian's and he was wearing a jacket that was very similar, too. 'Is this your brother, Julian?' she asked, though it was pretty obvious.

43

'Of course.' Julian put a firm, protective hand on Oliver's shoulder. 'Best brother in the world.'

Lucky was excited to finally meet her cousin. 'Hi,' she said to Oliver.

The boy started to smile, but then Julian whispered something in his ear and instead, Oliver frowned and stepped behind Julian.

Lucky was about to crack a joke to try to break the ice when Snips called out, 'I'll help Miss Cora carry cones!' Snips rushed towards the ice cream shop, where Cora had just pulled open the door. 'I'm coming, Miss Cora! Señor Carrots likes to share strawberry.'

Even though she couldn't see her aunt's face, Lucky could just imagine Cora's horrified expression at the idea of Snips and his donkey sharing an ice cream cone. Aunt Cora and Snips went into the shop, leaving Oliver with Julian.

'A deal's a deal.' Julian leaned over and wrote Oliver's name on the list before taking another long look. 'Here's my nine-year-old brother for your club this summer. You two are going to have a blast.'

'I didn't know Julian had a brother,' Abigail told Lucky while Julian was busy writing down the information.

'Is he nice?' Pru asked.

Lucky looked at Oliver, who pulled back farther into Julian's shadow. 'I've never met Oliver,' Lucky admitted. 'He's never come to town before now. Julian usually comes alone. I guess this summer Oliver is finally old enough to stay with Aunt Cora.' She glanced at the boy again, remembering how he'd frowned and pulled away from her. 'I don't really know if he's nice or not.'

Julian raised his head and set down the pen. 'Wait till you all get to know Oliver. He's

45

wonderful. I'm teaching him to be just like me.'

'That's adorable!' Abigail cooed. 'He'll grow up to be a little cousin Julian! So *classy*!'

Ugh. Lucky didn't think that was adorable. It sounded terrible, not good.

Julian tapped a finger on the sign-up sheet and told Lucky, 'I'm not paying yet.'

'Really? That's not how it works.' She stared at him. What was he up to? Everyone else paid half at sign-up, with the agreement they'd pay the other half at the end of the summer.

'Now, come on, Lucky! You know I'd never back out on a promise, especially to you! But I also promised my mum and Aunt Cora that little Oliver here would have a fun summer – and now I'm entrusting his happiness … to you. So before we get into the matter of payment, I want to make sure Oliver likes the club. It wouldn't be fair if he didn't have just as good of a time with you as he would've with his big brother, now would it? You gotta earn this money.' He patted his pocket again, which made Lucky wonder if he really did have two pounds in there.

Just then, Aunt Cora and Snips came out of the ice cream shop juggling cones for everyone. As they handed them out, Aunt Cora gushed to Lucky, 'It's going to be a wonderful summer.'

Lucky looked hard at Julian. 'Yes, it will be, Aunt Cora.' But she had some doubts. What if Oliver really was just like Julian? Someone like that, a mini-Julian con child, could ruin everything! Then again, they really did need the two pounds.

'Come, Oliver, time to unpack and settle in.' Aunt Cora led the way. Lucky noticed a spot of ice cream on Oliver's nose when he took one last long glance her way.

His expression was both cute and sad, kind of like a lost puppy. It looked to Lucky as if Oliver didn't want to be leaving with Cora. As if he wanted to stay with her and her friends. In that instant, Lucky felt her heart reach out towards him and she knew she was being given a big opportunity. This was about more than money!

She had a brilliant idea. Maybe if Oliver was around all summer, she could save him! Pru and Abigail and Lucky would make sure that Cousin Oliver turned out nothing like his sneaky older brother.

Lucky watched Oliver and her aunt walk to the corner, close to the place where the horses were enjoying some afternoon shade. Cora walked on, but Oliver paused to look at Spirit and let Julian catch up.

Then there was something odd that Lucky didn't understand. Julian seemed to hand Oliver something shiny from that money pocket of his. She saw the object glint in the sunlight before Oliver put it in his own pocket. Only then did they hurry after Cora. Weird; but everything about Julian was a little weird.

She cast aside her curiosity.

As her family turned and faded from view, Lucky was determined to make certain her new cousin had fun. She'd earn those two pounds and keep him far, far away from Julian's bad influence.

Diary Entry

I love when Aunt Cora comes over and cooks up a family dinner for us. The food is always amazing. Tonight, Cora made a new chicken pot pie recipe and I would have enjoyed it even more if things hadn't been so strange.

Oliver was super quiet, which was weird, but not the weirdest part.

It was Julian. He kept casting me strange looks across the table.

Aunt Cora, my dad and his new girlfriend, Kate (aka my teacher, Miss Flores), were all there and no one said anything about his odd expressions!

First, he'd peek over at Oliver, who was sitting in silence, picking at his food, but not eating much. Then he'd tip his head towards the door, as if that were some kind of signal. Then back at Oliver. Then Julian would tip his head to Cora. I swear, I thought his head would fall off his shoulders, if he kept going like that.

Finally, Aunt Cora noticed!

'Is everything okay, Julian?' Aunt Cora asked him. 'Do you have a neck ache?' She rose from the table. 'I have this lovely new balm I bought at the shop.'

I'd seen the balm on the counter. The label had said it could cure everything from aches and pains to chicken pox.

'No, no,' Julian said, rising from his own seat. 'Don't get up, Aunt Cora.' He put a hand on his neck, indicating that it really was the problem, and told her, 'Lucky can help me.'

I tried to protest. I wasn't done eating and the last thing I wanted was to be alone with Julian in the kitchen.

'Thanks, Cora,' my dad chimed in. 'Lucky, be sure to smear the balm all over his neck.'

Kate said, 'That's sure to help.'

'And give him a nice massage,' Aunt Cora added.

<u>Ugh! Yuck.</u> The worst part was I had no choice, because Con Boy Cousin was now holding his head in both hands and groaning, as if he were in pain.

'I'll show you pain,' I whispered and followed him into the kitchen.

'Ha!' Julian said once we were inside, letting go of his neck and rotating it freely. He popped up to sit on the counter. Aunt Cora would kill me if I did that. She probably wouldn't care if it was Julian, because he'd tell her some story about how his knees hurt and he couldn't stand. Or how he was helping me reach something high.

'I wanted to warn you about Oliver,' Julian said. 'He's not talking.'

'I noticed that,' I said. In fact, I hadn't heard him speak. Not on the street when we met and not yet at dinner.

'Well, I recommended he not speak to anyone but me until this club thing is

sorted out,' Julian said. 'I've given him
a little daily incentive to hold him to
it, too ... a penny a day.' He zipped his
lips. 'He's not supposed to say a
single word.'

Huh? What? I had no idea what was
going on.

'It's all part of making sure you
keep the PALs' fun club promise.' He
clicked his tongue. 'See, Oliver is a
nice kid. He'd probably tell you he was
having a great time all summer, just to
spare your feelings and then we'd never
really know if he was having any fun!
If he's just quiet, then we'll know for
sure. Now, I know it'll be a bit of
a challenge ... but aren't you up for
that, RF?'

I'm always up for a challenge, but this seemed unfair. 'How am I supposed to get him to have fun at the club if he won't talk?' Not talking? Not even grunting? Total silence? Uh, yeah, this is a problem. I can't ever trust Julian! He not only set me up to watch his brother all summer, but now he tells me he's paying Oliver not to talk!

'What are you up to?' I asked him.

He didn't reply. Instead, he said, 'It's all about having fun, right? This will make you work a little harder to make sure everyone has fun.' He smiled. 'I'm helping.'

That didn't seem like helping to me. 'What are you going to do while I'm working extra hard to make sure Oliver has fun?'

'I have ideas ...' Julian told me. Then he said, 'Don't forget, I'm only paying you if Oliver has a good time. If he talks, you'll know he's having fun. This way you might even know before I do.' He made that sound like a bonus.

That makes me wonder how he can afford to pay us at all, knowing he needs money for himself. I'll ask Pru and Abigail later, but what will we do if he never pays us? Knowing Julian, it's possible.

'So what do you have scheduled for the first day?' he asked me. There was a light in his eyes and I swear he was taking mental notes.

Abigail, Pru and I already have a list of activities and games ready. Because we love horses, we are using a lot of horse ideas.

'Prancing Ponies and a rodeo race. We've got a piñata that looks like a wild stallion and we're planning a blindfolded trust walk around bales of hay.' When I told him all that, Julian grinned. He said the club sounds 'Western Wonderful,' which makes me wonder if it isn't. Oh, he has snuck into my head and is confusing me! Did he mean it or not? What is he up to?

I'm working hard to shake my doubts away. No matter what Julian does, PALs Club is going to be so much fun that Oliver will forget his deal with Julian and start chatting — maybe he'll talk even more than Snips!

57

I'm determined to get Oliver to speak right away. I just have to show him that taking money from his brother is a bad idea. Being like Julian is another bad idea. I'm going to have to reverse that, and fast.

Julian jumped down from the counter and found Aunt Cora's balm. 'Glad we had this little talk,' he said, unscrewing the lid. '<u>Eww.</u> Stinky.' He took a big dollop and smeared it on his neck. Then he smeared some on my arm, so we smelled the same way: bad.

Before I could complain, he tossed the balm into my hands and said it was all part of the illusion, then dashed into the dining room.

He told Aunt Cora that I 'give a lovely massage' and have 'magic fingers.' But all I cared about was that I smelled awful and my dinner was cold.

Until Julian suggested I use the balm on Aunt Cora after dinner.

Julian! He'd conned everyone and now I couldn't refuse rubbing Cora's neck. 'Sure,' I said, giving him a side-eyed glance. He winked.

I knew that Oliver sat watching all this and I could see he was soaking it in. If I don't show him a good time at the club, he'll turn out exactly like Julian.
I have to stop that!

Project Save Oliver begins first thing in the morning.

CHAPTER 3

It was the first day of Adventure Club. Abigail was marking off names on a clipboard with a pencil.

'Club helper, Turo.' Abigail called out his name, even though he was standing right in front of her.

'Here,' he said, raising his hand. 'Ready to assist.'

'Mary Pat and Bianca?'

'Here,' they said in unison. They were dressed alike, with the exception of Bianca's blue boots and Mary Pat's brown boots – which was the only way to tell the twins apart.

'Snips?'

'And Señor Carrots reporting for duty.' Snips saluted.

'Lester?' New Kid One raised his hand.

'Lilly?' New Kid Two raised her hand. This was clearly Lester's younger sister. They both had choppy, wild brown hair. It looked as if they'd taken turns cutting each other's fringe.

'And, finally, Stella?'

A little girl, about nine years old, began to raise her hand, but then changed her mind. She raised her voice instead. 'I am here and ready for the club. If you don't mind, I have some suggestions. First, we are currently standing outside on the porch.' She indicated the horses milling nearby. 'I just think those animals are too close for comfort.'

Lucky laughed. 'Spirit is safe for—' she started.

'Wouldn't it be more comfortable for

everyone if we moved inside to the living room?' Stella asked before Lucky could finish.

'Pru is in the living room setting up for a scav—' Lucky began to explain.

Stella cut her off again. 'After our morning activity, Cook will be dropping my lunch. You'll need to invite her in to set the table for me. We'll be bringing our own silver, of course.'

'Are you related to Maricela?' Lucky asked.

'She's my second cousin once removed,' Stella declared. She held up two fingers and twisted them together. 'We're very close.'

'I'm sure you are …' Lucky said before turning to Abigail.

'Maricela and her family are away for a few weeks. They went to the city for important business,' Stella explained. 'My family is staying in their home. They'll be back soon, and we will spend the rest of the summer together.'

'I see,' Pru said, returning from the house. She approached Abigail and Lucky and whispered, 'That should be interesting. This town is only big enough for one Maricela!'

'And one Julian,' Lucky put in. They all laughed.

'That reminds me – we have just one last name …' Abigail looked around. 'Oliver?'

He wasn't there. She put an *x* by his name and set down the clipboard on the porch railing. 'Roll has been called. Now we can do our first activity.'

The kids all cheered.

'Wait,' Lucky said, stopping Abigail. 'What about Oliver?'

'I marked him absent,' Abigail said.

Just then, Julian arrived with Oliver. 'Girls,

I'm so sorry we're late,' Julian said. 'There were some details to work out this morning.' He gave his brother a small shove forward. 'He's here.'

'The club has already started,' Abigail said. 'Sorry.' She sounded very professional. 'Club policy. Come back tomorrow.'

'But he's here,' Julian said. He looked to Pru and Abigail. 'Be a pal, won't you, Abigail? What's this about a club policy?'

Pru shrugged. And Lucky looked blank. They had no clue what Abigail was talking about, but she had the clipboard, so she was in charge.

'Let me think what to do.' Abigail considered the problem. 'I suppose that we can give him a late pass for today.' She grabbed her clipboard and erased the x, putting a check by his name instead.

'Wow. She is strict,' Julian said to Lucky with a wink.

'Oliver had better be on time tomorrow,' Lucky said with a laugh. It always confused her a little when Julian seemed genuinely friendly.

Julian nodded, giving Oliver another little shove. 'See you later, little brother.'

Oliver didn't budge.

'You ready for fun, Oliver?' Abigail asked him.

He opened his mouth, then shut it quickly. Lucky watched as Julian slipped his brother a shiny penny. She'd already told Pru and Abigail about Julian's challenge. They were all determined to break Oliver's silence with a good time – and get paid.

'You ready for fun, Oliver?' Abigail asked him again.

This time, Oliver didn't even pretend to

try to answer. He kept his lips pressed tightly together.

'It's okay, Abigail,' Lucky said. 'I've got this.' She reached out to take Oliver's hand. He shoved it away. She frowned and addressed all the waiting kids. 'Now, where were we? Ah yes, who's prepared for the best scavenger hunt *ever*?'

Julian looked at Lucky and winked. 'Go on,' he told Oliver. 'I'll pick you up later. You know what to do.'

Oliver gave his brother a serious look and held out his hand.

'You're getting more like me every day, kid.' With a sigh, Julian pressed a second penny into his palm. 'I'm very proud.' Then to Lucky, Julian said, 'Well, I'm off to do important grown-up things.'

'You're fourteen,' Lucky reminded her cousin.

'Almost fifteen,' Julian corrected her. He took a giant step away from Oliver. 'Have fun.'

Oliver shook his head, refusing the idea.

'Then don't have any fun,' Julian said, smiling. 'You'll save me two pounds.'

Lucky had to stop this madness. How had she gotten tricked into taking a kid who refused to talk, didn't want to have fun so his brother wouldn't have to pay her and was getting paid pennys for his sabotage?

Two pounds, she reminded herself. They all wanted the money. Plus, there was the chance to save Oliver from being like Julian. She puffed out her chest and announced in a cheerful voice, 'Come on! The scavenger hunt starts inside.'

Oliver gave one last look at Julian, then followed Lucky inside, where the kids were getting their instructions.

'The scavenger hunt is starting!' Pru broke the kids into groups. Turo took Lester and Lilly in his group. Snips, Stella, Mary Pat and Bianca were in the other.

'Oh goody,' Bianca said, sidling up close to Snips. Mary Pat scoffed and stuck out her tongue at the sight.

Snips moved away from them both. 'I think I should be on Oliver's team,' he said, noticing that Oliver still didn't have a team. 'We could be a two-man crew. The mighty Club Comrades.' Snips went and linked arms with Oliver, who didn't protest. 'Just the two of us, against the world.'

'Ah shucks,' Bianca said when Pru agreed to the group change. She blew a kiss to Snips. 'See you at the finish line, sweetie.'

Snips rolled his eyes. 'Not if we're there first.'

That made no sense to Lucky, but Snips hardly ever did.

'Okay then, we have three teams.' Pru handed each group an envelope and an empty grain bag. 'You need to find one of each thing on the list. Winners get an extra piece of the cherry pie that Abigail's grandma made for dessert.' It was the first day of the club. The PALs wanted to start off the week by impressing the kids with their best prize – there was nothing better than Grandma Stone's pies.

'I won't be eating the pie,' Stella announced. 'Cook will bring me my own dessert. So what do I get if I win?'

'Your *team*, you mean,' Pru said. 'What will your *team* get?'

'Sure,' Stella said, frowning at Mary Pat and Bianca. 'Them.'

'We want the pie,' Mary Pat countered. 'Mrs Stone's pie is famous in Miradero. Don't change the prize,' she begged Lucky.

'The prize stays,' Lucky agreed. 'Sorry, Stella.'

Stella grumped. 'My aunt will hear about this later.'

Abigail had a small copper bell. 'When I ring the bell, the hunt is on.'

Lucky looked straight at Oliver. 'Have a fun adventure,' she said and winked.

He pinched his lips together and didn't say anything. Snips still had his arm looped through Oliver's. 'Come on, Ollie, we gotta win us some pie.'

The bell rang and each team opened their lists.

On the paper were things that should've been easy to find:

Riding boots

A round rock

A green leaf

A horse bridle

Something red

A hoof pick

A summer flower

An old newspaper

A grooming brush

Since the kids could go anywhere in Miradero to find things, the PALs followed the groups on their horses. Every time Lucky passed by Oliver, she could see him staring at Spirit. It looked as if Oliver really wanted to ride a horse.

Lucky pulled alongside him and Snips as they were about to pluck a flower from old Mrs Gerstein's garden.

'I wouldn't do that,' Lucky warned them.

'How are we supposed to get a dumb flower if we can't pick one?' Snips asked. He sneezed. 'I hate flowers.'

'Go ask Mrs Gerstein,' Lucky said. The secret was that she, Abigail and Pru had already visited several homes and asked if the kids could pick flowers. That meant if they asked, the answer would be yes. If they didn't ask permission, their team would be disqualified from the pie prize.

Suddenly, Spirit reared back. There was a bee and he swished his tail at it, snorting and huffing for it to go away.

'Calm down, boy,' Lucky said, holding on for the wild ride. 'It's just a baby bumblebee. It's looking for a pollen snack.'

Spirit relaxed and the bee flew off towards a flower in the garden.

When Lucky looked back at Oliver, his face was flushed.

'The bee's gone,' she told him. He shook his head. 'Then what?' Lucky prodded gently. 'Why do you look so scared?'

Oliver shook his head again.

'Come on, Oliver,' Lucky said as nicely as she could. 'Julian isn't around. You can tell me.'

Snips stepped up to his new friend. 'He's afraid of you, Lucky,' Snips teased. He grabbed Oliver's wrist. 'Come on, Ollie. You don't have to talk to her. Or me. Or anyone. Just be yourself.' He tugged Oliver along. 'Let's go ask Mrs Gerstein for a flower. She might give us a cookie, too. She's nice like that ...' Oliver glanced back at Lucky and Spirit as Snips dragged him away.

When they all got back to the club, Pru collected each team's bag and went through the items. Abigail, Pru and Lucky had agreed when they'd first planned the scavenger hunt that it wasn't going to be truly competitive. This first one was about team building and having an amazing day.

'The winner,' Pru announced at the end of lunch, 'is *everyone*!'

All the kids cheered.

Abigail brought out a second serving of pie for all the kids, even Stella.

'I guess the first piece was pretty okay,' she said, licking her lips. 'I think I should see if the second is any better. I mean, the recipe might be the same, but it's a different pie ... technically.'

Pru stood on a chair. 'I'm surprised. No one missed anything on the list.' That was intentional. She playfully scratched her chin. 'Tomorrow, I'll make it harder.'

The first day had done exactly what they

wanted it to. Build confidence. Be fun. Get everyone into the activities. It might not have been the most 'adventurous' activity, but Lucky thought it was a huge success.

'Add carrots to the hunt,' Snips suggested. 'I'll bring Señor Carrots.'

From near the front of Lucky's house, she heard Señor Carrots bray with a loud *hee-haw*.

After lunch they played Prancing Ponies and had a horseshoe toss. Through it all, Oliver stuck to Snips. In the Ponies game, when Lilly ran between the boys, trying to break their arm link apart, Oliver held tightly, until Lilly gave up and crawled under.

'Cheater,' Snips said.

'Nu-uh,' Lilly told him. 'This is how we play in the city.'

'The city is wrong, then,' Snips challenged. 'Miradero is the best.' He turned to Oliver.

'What are the Prancing Pony rules where you're from?'

Oliver didn't reply, so Snips told Lilly, 'Oliver agrees. You have to break through our grips or you're out.' He let go of Oliver's hand and dramatically shouted. *'Out!'*

Just then, one of the twins barrelled through the gap in the boys' hands and cheered when she reached the other side safely. 'Gotcha!'

'I've been Bianca'ed,' Snips moaned. 'She's a tricky one.'

Lucky thought she saw Oliver laugh at the silliness, but she wasn't positive.

When Julian arrived to walk Oliver back to Cora's, he asked, 'How was club, big guy?'

Oliver leaned in and whispered something to Julian, who said loudly, 'Are you sure?'

Oliver nodded. Julian whispered something

back, then Oliver whispered something else to Julian.

Lucky was almost sure he said, 'Fun,' but then in a voice Lucky, Pru and Abigail could all hear, Oliver told Julian, 'It was *boring*.'

It was the first and only thing Oliver said that Lucky had heard.

Right after that announcement, Oliver walked away with Julian. Julian replied loudly, clearly intending for his voice to carry. 'There wasn't any adventure at adventure club? How disappointing that must have been for you, Oliver. I'm sorry old RF let you down.'

Lucky wondered whether other kids agreed. As parents came to get them, Lucky could hear funny stories about extra pie and cheating at games, but Oliver might've been right: the easy scavenger hunt, the pie prize for everyone, the games ... It'd all been part of the plan, but maybe there really wasn't enough adventure in adventure club. If she wanted to break through to Oliver, without having to pay him herself, something had to change.

At sunset, the PALs went for a ride to talk about the club schedule for the next day. They galloped to a large, open field where they could see for miles in every direction, and they stopped to rest. The sunset cast a golden hue over the summer sky.

'I think Julian is right,' Lucky said, surprised that she agreed with him. 'We need more excitement at the club.'

'Tomorrow's scavenger hunt list has a pinecone on it,' Pru said. 'That shouldn't be easy to find in the summertime and after lunch we can make the pinecones into bird feeders.'

'Fun,' Abigail agreed. 'I made a bird feeder last summer. A cute little bluebird came. Then Snips scared it away.' She sighed. 'No birds ever came after that. None were brave enough to face off with Snips.'

'Sounds … not very adventurous,' Lucky said. But then she had an idea. It came to her after seeing the way that Oliver looked at Spirit. 'Instead of horse games, can we change to having a *real* horse adventure club tomorrow?' she asked Pru and Abigail. She added, 'Actually, not just for tomorrow. Can we change the whole club?'

Pru considered the idea. 'Scavenger hunts around the barn?'

'That wasn't what I was thinking,' Lucky said. 'Instead of a scavenger hunt, maybe we can have a treasure hunt on horseback. We could learn rope tricks and animal tracking.'

Pru loved tracking and was really good at it.

'I'm in,' Pru said. 'Horses! Adventure!'

'You don't have to convince me,' Abigail agreed.

'The PALs Summer Adventure Horse Club starts tomorrow!' Lucky announced and the girls cheered before mounting up and racing back home.

✦Diary Entry✦

There's no better place for me
to think than sitting on Spirit's back.

We went for a walk — slowly, so I
could talk and write in my diary as
we went along. Spirit doesn't talk
much, but he sure is a good listener.

Here's the problem:

Oliver is a pain! He won't do anything.
It is so aggravating. I mean, seriously,
he just sits and stares out towards
the horizon all day. I'm not saying he
ruined the day, but ... he sort of did.

All the kids were so excited about
going to the barn, except Oliver.

And Stella. She announced that horses were dirty and smelly, but then seeing that everyone else was having fun, she quietly asked if she could ride a small spotted mare named Sadie. After Pru showed her how to mount the horse and walk slowly in a circle, we couldn't get Stella out of the saddle so Mary Pat could ride! I'll bet that Stella's at Maricela's house right now, writing a letter to her parents asking for a horse of her very own.

Oliver, however, is a problem. I have no idea what I should do with him! For a kid who loves adventure, he sure doesn't want to have one. He's still not talking, except to Julian, and even then the only word I ever overhear is <u>boring</u>.

Pru suggested we ignore 'Mr Boring Pants' and let him sit by a tree, which is where he'd planted himself. She said we had other kids who wanted to have fun, so why should we bother with the <u>one</u> who refused to even try? She pointed out that even Stella was having fun.

When I asked Abigail what to do, she thought we should get Julian to come help us. It was obvious that he hadn't found a job, or wasn't trying very hard to get one, because we could see him in the distance, climbing rocks. All that stuff about how he didn't like adventure seemed like a wild tale, since every once in a while we'd hear him shout 'Wahoo!' as if he were having the best time ever.

Oliver watched his brother with eagle eyes. That was one of the issues. He couldn't ride a horse because he couldn't stop watching Julian doing whatever Julian was doing. As it was, we had to keep the other kids from getting distracted and watching Julian, too.

There was no way I'd have my cousin come to club now, not even if it was the only way to get Oliver involved. No chance. I told Abigail that and she was disappointed. She doesn't have the same issues with trusting Julian that I do.

I also told Pru that ignoring Oliver wasn't going to work, either. He is my cousin and my responsibility. My goal is still to get him to stop looking at

Julian, and start focussing here. He is going to have fun!

I am not losing this challenge! No way.

But what should I do? It was Spirit who had the answer. I was so wrapped up in my thoughts, I hadn't noticed where we were headed. When I realised which trail we were on, the biggest idea came to me!

I turned Spirit away from the trailhead. We weren't going to go down that way right then — but we sure could <u>later</u>!

Julian says that Oliver likes only adventure? Okay, we'll give him an adventure! <u>Extra Awesome Horse Adventure!</u>

CHAPTER 4

'*Adventure* doesn't mean *danger*,' Pru said. The PALs were getting the kids acquainted with their horses at a riding ring near Miradero's main square and Lucky had suggested a ride out to Dusty Dan's grave site. To get there, they'd have to ride the same way that Spirit had taken her the day before, then continue through Thin Man's Canyon and cross Wild Wanda's Creek. They'd all been on that ride before. It was one of the most fun rides in Miradero, but there were spots that just weren't safe for beginning riders.

'If the rumours are true and Dan is buried near all the gold coins that he stole from the stagecoaches he robbed, we could make a treasure hunt out of the trip,' Lucky suggested. She had it all worked out. They'd break into three groups, each one with a PAL and her horse. 'Spirit and I will lead the more advanced riders,' she explained, adding, 'We can even take our lunch bags and picnic by the creek.'

'No can do,' Pru countered. 'It's too far, Lucky. We have kids who are just learning to ride.' She pointed over at Stella, who'd brought an apple for Sadie, but was too scared to hand it to her. Every time Sadie ducked her head to take it from Stella's hand, the girl squealed and jumped back, snatching away the apple. If that 'game' didn't end soon, Stella would find out what happens when you tease a hungry horse.

'I'll be right back,' Pru said with a sigh. She went over to help Stella by showing her how to hold her hand out flat. Lucky could see that Stella closed her eyes and didn't breathe until Sadie took the apple. Of course, afterward she cheered and said, 'I want to do it again!' Turned out Stella had brought a whole bag of apples. Spirit and the other horses started to gather around for her to feed them, too.

Pru glanced at Lucky and Abigail. Her expression said two things:

This could take a while.

Don't you dare decide to go to Dusty Dan's grave.

'Pru's being an adventure killer,' Lucky complained to Abigail, half joking. 'If we don't do something wild, how am I going to win over my little cousin?' Oliver was back under the same tree where he'd spent the entire week so far.

Abigail and Lucky looked over at him.

He was wearing clean blue overalls and gazing out towards a shadowed figure in the distance.

'Is that Julian?' Abigail asked, raising her hand to shield her eyes and squinting into the sunlight.

The figure waved at them and they could see he was carrying fishing poles and a tackle box. It was Julian for certain.

'Looks as if he's headed to Wild Wanda's Creek today,' Abigail noted. 'I once caught a fish there that was as big as my own head.' She put her hands on her ears, then steadily moved them forward. Studying the distance between her palms, she nodded. 'Yep, that's how big it was.'

'Sure,' Lucky said. She'd seen the fish and it hadn't been very big at all. 'We could go fishing, too.'

'Exactly,' Abigail said. 'Let's team up with Julian. He seems to be having a lot of fun.'

'I know,' Lucky said, pinching together her lips thoughtfully. 'But he told me he was getting a job, not rock climbing, hiking, flying a kite and now fishing.' Those were all things they'd seen him doing. Lucky stared out at her cousin. 'Something is fishy, that's for sure.'

'You made a fin-tastic joke!' Abigail cheered.

They both laughed.

Spirit came over to Abigail. He was chewing on one of Stella's apples. 'Come on, Spirit,' Lucky said. 'Let's see if we can get Oliver to ride today.'

Abigail went to help the others saddle up for turns around the ring, while Pru was still with Stella, who squealed – this time with joy – every time a horse ate an apple. Boomerang and Chica Linda had their mouths full, chomping happily.

Oliver seemed to brighten when he saw Spirit. 'Hey, cuz,' Lucky greeted. 'Want to feed Spirit an apple?'

Oliver seemed to consider it for a long moment, but then shook his head.

'What? Not adventurous enough for you?' She got a glint in her eye and called over to Pru, 'Can I have a couple of those apples?'

'Sure,' Pru replied and Turo carried over a few.

'What are you up to, Lucky?' Turo asked her.

'Adding a little adventure,' she said with a smile.

Lucky urged Oliver to stand up. 'Can you throw?'

She showed him what she meant. Lucky lobbed an apple through the air, as hard and

as far as she could. The instant the apple
left her fingers, Spirit took off running. He
galloped over the open field to snag the
apple midair!

The kids, who'd all stopped to watch,
clapped and hooted.

'Now your turn,' Lucky said, handing
Oliver an apple.

Oliver didn't look like a strong shot, so
Lucky called Spirit to come in closer and she
positioned him partway between Oliver and
the town square. As it turned out, Oliver had
a good arm but a really bad aim. He tossed
the apple hard and it flew way over Spirit's
head, towards Main Street, where people were
milling about.

'Oh no! Oliver!' Lucky shouted as the
apple flew towards a street vendor with a cart
of pots and pans. She called to him, 'Duck!'

'Huh?' The old man didn't move very

fast. The apple was coming in hard, straight towards his surprised face.

In a flash, Spirit leaped over two young women eating at an outside café, snagged the apple and skidded to a stop, catching himself just in time before crashing into the bakery.

'Good boy, Spirit!' Lucky shouted, chasing after her horse.

He was in the street, where a small group came to see what had happened.

'That horse is a menace,' a young man told his wife loudly enough that others could hear.

'Vote for me for mayor and we will keep wild horses out of the main square,' a man in a hat called out. He was running against Maricela's father for the job.

'That horse tried to kill me,' one of the women from the café added to the throng.

'Come on, Spirit,' Lucky said, leading her

horse away. 'I know you were just trying to protect the street vendor.'

As they passed the man with the pots and pans cart, he thanked them, then turned to the angry mob, trying to explain, but no one would listen.

Lucky climbed on Spirit's back. She was going to try to explain to the group. 'I'm so sorry,' she said. 'We—'

'Don't let it happen again!' the man running for mayor interrupted, then began handing out flyers for the upcoming election. Everyone turned away, interested in hearing the man's plans to keep wild horses off the streets.

When she and Spirit got back to the others, Oliver had all the kids gathered around him. All of a sudden, he was chatting up a storm.

'Did you see my toss?' he was bragging to

Snips. 'I'd have hit one of those hanging pots if it weren't for that wild horse.'

He glanced up, sensing Spirit was behind him, and moved a few steps away.

'*That wild horse* saved the old man from a bump on the head,' Lucky countered. 'What were you thinking?' *Wait!* Oliver was talking. Bragging, actually, but at least he had words coming from his mouth. It seemed that all it took to get Oliver talking was bad behaviour. Maybe he was finally loving the club!

'Why are you talking?' Lucky asked him. She wondered if things were easier when he wasn't speaking at all.

'Because I've decided that the club is so boring,' Oliver told her in a droll, Julian-like voice. 'I told Julian that he won the challenge. Next week, I'm not coming to Adventure Club anymore.'

That explained it. He didn't have a reason to keep silent. In Oliver's eyes, Julian had won. Problem was, if Oliver didn't come back, Lucky and her friends would be out two pounds. They needed that money.

What to do?

Once he started speaking, it was hard to get him to stop. And Lucky would've loved for him to stop. 'We could be having so much more fun if there was a little more *danger*,' said Oliver.

Abigail leaned to Lucky and said, 'He sounds a lot like Julian, doesn't he?'

'That's what I've been trying to prevent,' Lucky said, moaning.

She went back to the idea that Oliver liked adventure. Wasn't that why he threw the apple? To mix things up and see what would happen?

Oliver was still talking and now he had the

ears of all the kids. And it looked as
if they agreed with him!

'My brother would make this club much
more fun,' he told them all.

'We remember the roller coaster,' Turo
said. 'That was amazing.'

'But he stole all your money,' Lucky
reminded everyone. 'Julian is not the
answer.'

'Ten minutes ago everything was fine. No
one was complaining about the club before
you started talking,' Pru told Oliver. She
pointed at his tree. 'You can go sit down now.'

'No!' Snips argued. 'We want to hear what
Ollie wants to do.'

Abigail, who had been supportive of Julian
coming to the club, said, 'Maybe we could
just ask Julian for a few fun ideas.'

'No,' Lucky protested. 'Never.' This was
a nightmare and Oliver, rapidly becoming

Julian Junior, was turning the kids against the
PALs. He wouldn't stop talking – and none
of it was in support of the PALs Awesome
Adventure Club.

'We want more fun,' Mary Pat and Bianca
cried.

'Want to throw more apples at town?' Stella
asked with a glint in her eye. 'I think Maricela
would be okay if we used the guy running
against her dad for mayor as target practice.'

This was all getting out of hand. The kids
were rebelling. Now they were chanting
'Bor-ring!' over and over.

The day was almost done. Lucky had to
do something, or no one would come back to
the club after the weekend. And worse, they
might request their money back. How would
Lucky explain to Aunt Cora when she couldn't
replace the crystal bottle and the bubble bath?

'I know!' Lucky said, and turned to her friends. 'Let's have an O-Mok-See.'

'O-Mok-Fun!' Abigail said. An O-Mok-See was like a rodeo, but with more fun games and less competition.

'That sounds great!' Pru agreed. 'Safe adventure and a lot of fun.'

They all put their hands in a pile and raised them together, shouting, 'O-Mok-See!'

The kids wanted to know what that meant, and Abigail said with a chuckle, 'O-You'll-See.'

Everyone was intrigued, but soon Oliver declared, 'You have no fun ideas. It'll be boring just like everything else.' He mocked them, saying, 'How about we have another scavenger hunt? Everyone can find dirt and rocks! Winner gets pie, because that's the only prizes we have and everyone wins because there's no real competition.'

'Oliver—' Lucky began. This wasn't fair.

He was ruining the club. Hadn't she predicted this from the start?

Just then the parents started to arrive and pick up the kids. Julian whistled from across the riding ring and Oliver took off running.

Lucky watched her cousins leave and sighed. Oliver might not show up next week, but he was going to regret it. The kids were going to have so much fun that he'd be begging Julian to let him come back. And not just that, he'd offer to pay *three* pounds for the privilege.

The PALs Summer Adventure Horse Club was about to get more adventurous.

Diary Entry

I am keeping my diary with me at all times because strange things are happening and I don't want to forget any of them.

First, today, Abigail told me that she can't find her club roll-call list. That isn't weird by itself, but other things are happening, too, that make it highly suspicious. I feel like Boxcar Bonnie, super sleuth and star of my favourite mystery book series, getting the sniff of a mystery.

Second, I saw the kids from Adventure Club hanging out together

in the town square. I was surprised
to discover it was all of them at the
same time. They looked as if they were
having a serious conversation. When I
went by to say 'Hi,' and see what was
going on, they scattered as if they
shouldn't have been there at all. Even
Stella hurried away and I would have
thought she'd have stayed around to
tell me everything that was wrong
with the club and what she'd like to
see improved when we met up again on
Monday.

Third, as I rode to where Abigail and
Pru were meeting me, I noticed Julian
coming out of the supermarket. Actually,
Spirit saw him first and pointed him
out. Gotta give Spirit credit — he's like a
watch-horse sometimes!

It was then that I saw Oliver hurry over to Julian. That was odd because I'd also seen Oliver a few minutes earlier with the other kids. Oliver talked to Julian and pointed at the kids; then the two of them went to where the kids were standing around. They all gathered around Julian while he stood in the middle, talking in a low voice that I couldn't hear.

I didn't understand. Why would Julian be hanging out at a kids meeting? What was going on?

I had many questions, but no time to figure out the answers. I was late to meet up with Abigail and Pru. When I got to the barn, I told them that my cousin was acting suspiciously.

Pru reined back Chica Linda to a walk, so we could speak. Abigail turned sidesaddle on Boomerang and told us she thought it was nice that Oliver was hanging out with the other kids. She even suggested that he might participate in the O-Mok-See at the club on Monday.

I hope he'll get involved.

Pru was worried that we're starting to focus too much on just one kid. She was mad about the whole apple thing and I had to agree with her.

There was something strange happening that I couldn't put my finger on ...

Spirit interrupted our serious talk with a loud neigh. I followed his eyes and could see several small dots on the horizon.

'Are those our kids?' Pru asked, cupping her hands like binoculars and looking through.

'That's nice,' Abigail said. 'They want to hang out so much that they aren't even taking a day off.'

'I think Julian is leading them to the rocky outcrop,' Pru said.

The rocky outcrop is a forbidden canyon wall. The huge rocks and boulders are stacked like marbles, stretched high towards a high cliff edge. They look fun to climb, but the boulders aren't secure. Rock slides happen pretty often and since the rocks are big and heavy, the area's considered very dangerous.

We spurred our horses into a gallop and took off to see what was going on.

Pru was right. Julian was leading and he had the entire club with him. Not just that, but I could see he had Abigail's roster as well. It was folded and sticking out of his shirt pocket, but there was no mistaking Abigail's handwriting.

I was so mad that I shouted at him instead of asking politely what he was doing.

Julian didn't flinch. He calmly thanked Abigail for the list and offered to give it back to her.

She took it, but we all knew she hadn't given it to him.

'It took an extra penny, but Oliver brought it home,' Julian explained as if it were no big deal. I realised I'd seen the payoff the first day of the club. It must have taken Oliver time to snag the list when Abigail wasn't looking. 'How else was I going to contact the kids for Julian's Giant Adventure Club?'

I thought Pru was going to jump off Chica Linda and strangle my cousin.

'Those are our kids,' she told Julian, her voice gritty with anger.

'Not anymore,' Julian said with a chuckle. 'The kids have spoken – and they're saying your club is, well, a bit dull. So I decided to host my own better club.' I realised that he'd been planning this since the day he'd come to town. Boxcar Bonnie would've told me the clues were there all along. She's such a great detective. It just took me all this time to realise that

Julian never intended to pay us two pounds. He'd said he had a job plan the moment I told him there were no openings in town. He'd meant he'd be taking our job.

He'd said he'd pay us, then paid Oliver instead, knowing that without talking, Oliver – the chattiest kid on the planet – would have a terrible time. That meant he'd never have to pay us. He'd paid Oliver to ruin the club for the others and then paid him to steal our sign-up sheet.

He'd used his brother to convince the other kids to switch clubs.

This was Julian at his worst. He'd conned us all! And still, here the kids thought he was just more fun and they liked that.

'You see, the truth is, no one likes
your club. Your club doesn't have
enough adventure,' Julian explained.
'Mine will be double the danger and
double the fun.' He pointed to the rocky
outcrop up ahead. 'Today's a free trial
day and if they like it, they can come
to my club instead of yours on Monday.'

'You're a club stealer!' I argued.

'No, I'm a businessman,' Julian said.
'You and your friends had a great
idea ... I just made it better. So don't
be mad, RF. It's all for the benefit of
the <u>kids</u>. And when they all like my
club better, you can just transfer the
money the kids already paid you — to
me.' He patted that pants pocket of his.
Now I <u>knew</u> it was empty. 'I'll take care
of the finances from here on.'

'Imitation is the best form of flattery,' Abigail said halfheartedly.

Pru grunted at her.

'Not only did I promise my mum I'd get a job, but with all these kids, and only one counsellor' – he pointed to himself – 'I can get her a gift with my earnings. There's this beautiful crystal bubble bath bottle in the supermarket that I'd like to buy.'

'No, no, no!' I couldn't believe he was that cruel. 'That's mine!' I said. He knew about the bubble bath and he knew that was why I needed to earn enough to buy a new bottle. I was back to yelling. 'I'm getting that bottle for Aunt Cora!'

'It's not my fault you didn't succeed.' Julian shrugged innocently. 'When you pass the money to me and the kids have fun, you can brag about how you helped launch my fabulous club.'

Every memory I had that made me think Julian was a decent guy disappeared. 'You're awful,' I told him.

'Awful-ly fun!' he said, encouraging the kids to all laugh at his joke.

'Oliver?' I looked at my little cousin. 'Please don't turn out like Julian.'

Oliver grinned happily. 'But I want to be just like him,' he said. 'My brother's going to have the best club in all of Miradero.'

I threw up my hands. It was too late. Oliver was a mini-Julian!

The group moved forward, leaving me, Pru and Abigail behind.

What were we going to do?

Pru stepped up. 'We have to stop them from going to the rocky outcrop. Not only is Julian a club-napper, but it's too dangerous.'

The battle had begun. This was war. I galloped on Spirit until I was side by side with my cousin. I climbed off Spirit and stepped close, nose to nose with Julian.

'<u>Are you</u> up for a <u>challenge</u>?' I asked, repeating the way he'd asked me earlier.

'Possibly.' Julian stopped and turned, intrigued. 'What do you have in mind?'

I said, 'We'll have PALs Adventure Club in the morning on Monday with the O-Mok-See and you could have your Julian club in the afternoon, after lunch.'

'And the kids will vote?' Julian asked, getting into the idea.

'Yes,' I agreed. 'Whoever has the best day at their club will win the kids, their payment and the right to buy the crystal bottle. It's an all-or-nothing contest.'

'Done,' he said.

'Fine,' I agreed.

We shook hands.

Pru and Abigail couldn't believe what happened, but I figure I saved the day. Just as Pru wanted — no one was going to the forbidden rocky outcrop. At least not that very minute.

Of course, now we have a new challenge. We have to work hard to win the kids over, have fun <u>and</u> convince Oliver that his brother is nobody's hero.

Our old club is not going to be enough. We have to throw out everything we've done and start fresh. New games. New prizes. New ideas.

It'll be difficult, but the PALs are going to throw the best O-Mok-See that Miradero has ever seen.

CHAPTER 5

'Did you know the word *O-Mok-See* is from a Native American tradition where warriors would dance before going out to battle?' Abigail was explaining to the kids what we would be doing that day. 'The warriors would get all dressed up.' She pointed to a basket of hats and costumes the girls had collected.

'And they'd paint their horses.' Pru demonstrated by using chalk paint to draw a lightning bolt on Chica Linda.

Lucky added to the story. 'The warriors would carry shields and spears.'

'Can we have spears?' Lester asked.

'Uh, maybe paper ones ...' Pru said.

'Boring.' Oliver yawned. He was clearly still trying to help Julian turn the kids against the PALs.

'I don't think that spears and dancing mix well. In fact, that sounds very unsafe to me,' Stella protested.

'I have to agree,' Pru said, looking at Bianca and Mary Pat, who were already pretending to stab each other and staging dramatic deaths.

'Oh, you got me good,' Bianca moaned, flopping to the ground.

'You got me, too.' Mary Pat crashed on top of her sister.

Bianca raised her head. 'Save us, Snips …'

'No thanks.' Snips turned away. He asked Abigail, 'Can I paint Señor Carrots so he's ready for the battle?'

'Of course,' Abigail said. 'All the horses will get symbols before we ride.'

'Cool,' Snips said. 'I'm going to paint carrots on the señor.'

Bianca and Mary Pat sat up. 'That's silly,' Mary Pat said.

'But adorable,' Bianca said.

Snips groaned.

'Okay, kids,' Lucky said. 'We are going to get ready for the O-Mok-See and then we will compete!'

There wasn't a lot of time to get everything done before Julian got his turn, so the kids hurried to get costumes and to paint.

'We should have spears,' Oliver muttered as he passed Lucky. 'Sharp, pointy ones.'

'I'd like to spear him,' Pru said. 'Right in his complaining—'

'You can't spear the children,' Abigail said matter-of-factly, then noticed that the kids who were supposed to be painting Boomerang were actually throwing the chalky

117

paint at one another. She looked at Pru and Lucky. 'Do either of you have a spear?'

Lucky laughed.

The girls went to where some kids were picking out costumes.

Turo helped Lester tie a bandana around his neck. 'There,' he said, admiring his work. 'You look like a fine cowboy.'

Lester tore off the bandana. 'I'm supposed to be a pirate, not a cowboy.'

'Be whatever you want,' Turo said, giving up.

'I'm going to dress as Stella, cousin of Maricela of Miradero,' Stella announced proudly, refusing even to look through the costumes.

'You sure you don't want this bonnet?' Pru said, holding up a frilly pink hat with lace strings that belonged to her grandmother. 'It's pretty.'

'No thank you,' Stella said, but then when

Lilly started looking at it, she changed her mind, put it on and smiled. 'I'd like to wear it, actually.'

Lilly took a fur trader's hat instead.

Snips smeared mud on his face and arms and said, 'I'll be a pig. Surely there were pigs at the warrior parties.'

'Maybe for dinner,' Pru whispered to Lucky, who giggled.

'That costume suits you, Snips,' Abigail told her brother. 'You did eat five eggs for breakfast.' She'd been late downstairs, and he'd eaten both his breakfast and hers!

'Oink,' Snips replied sassily.

They moved on to painting the horses.

Spirit was very patient as several kids decorated him with handprints and lightning bolts and words like *Good Luck* and *Fly Fast*.

'Who drew a bunch of carrots on Spirit?' Lucky asked, looking straight at Snips.

'Uh, I don't know.' Snips turned away, digging the toe of his shoe in the dirt and whistling, before bursting into a giggle fit and running away. He made sure Señor Carrots was always front and centre.

Everyone was having a good time – except Oliver, of course – but was it enough to make them stay in the PALs' club?

Aunt Cora came by, obviously unaware of the trouble her nephews were causing, with a tray of horse-shaped cookies.

'Let's take a break!' Lucky told the kids, who were now in costumes and covered with paint. It looked as if there was more paint on the kids than any of the horses. They all left their horses behind to gather around for cookies.

'Thanks, Aunt Cora,' Lucky said, picking a cookie that looked a lot like Spirit. She took a bite and muttered through crumbs, '*Mmm. Delicious.*'

'You can thank Julian for the idea,' Aunt Cora said. 'He thought you all would like a snack.'

'Julian?' Pru asked, nearly choking on a bite of Chica Linda–looking cookie.

'He's so thoughtful,' Abigail said, but then corrected, 'I mean, he's thinking all right, but what's he thinking about?' She put a finger against her temple. 'It boggles the mind.'

Lucky swallowed hard. It felt as if the cookie were suddenly caught in her throat. 'What is he up to?' she asked herself. Then to Aunt Cora, she asked, 'Where is Julian? I'd love to thank him for his role in this delightful idea.'

'He was here a moment ago.' Cora lowered the tray so Snips could get a second cookie. Holding the tray steady, she looked over her shoulder. Julian wasn't there. She glanced over her other shoulder, then turned completely around. 'I don't know. I suppose it's possible he went to get the children drinks to go with the cookies.'

'I *am* thirsty,' Abigail said.

'That would be nice of him,' Lucky agreed, 'but there's no way.' She was fully convinced he was up to something. But what?!

They had only another hour before the kids went to Julian's Con Boy Club, so Lucky said, 'Thank you so much, Aunt Cora, for the treats.' Then she announced to the kids, 'Time to ride!' There were several events in a traditional O-Mok-See and they were determined to do as many as possible before lunch. 'Let's go!'

She really hoped that Oliver would get involved. But so far, it wasn't looking good.

Speaking of Oliver ...

Lucky asked Pru and Abigail, 'Have you seen Julian Junior?' She was kidding, but it turned out to be a nickname that fit!

While they'd been having cookies with Cora, Julian and Oliver had been working on their own project. The two appeared around the corner of the barn with sneaky grins on their faces, leading the horses behind them.

'I cleaned the horses for you,' Julian said, as if that were a good thing. He indicated Spirit. 'That one refused to be washed, but the others enjoyed it very much.'

The way he said it made Lucky wonder if Oliver had actually helped him, or if this betrayal was all Julian's doing. All the horses looked just like they had at the beginning of the day. None of them had any festive paint on them anymore. She felt as if her blood might boil right out of her skin.

'It's not the horses' fault. Boomerang loves a bath when it's not lavender-y,' Abigail said. 'Julian tricked us.'

Lucky, with Pru and Abigail on her heels, marched up to where Julian was putting away the bucket and brushes.

'You had Aunt Cora bring cookies so you could distract us,' Lucky accused him.

'Is that anyway to thank me?' Julian replied. 'I had Aunt Cora bring the kids some delicious treats and I washed the horses.' He set down the bucket. His shirt was all wet. 'You're welcome.'

'You knew the horses were painted for the O-Mok-See!' Pru poked Julian in the chest with a finger. 'You're trying to ruin everything so your club is more fun.'

'No,' Julian countered. 'My club will be more fun because going to Dusty Dan's grave will be much more of an adventure than

124

riding around a few barrels on a painted' – he paused – 'on a nice clean horse.'

'Ugh!' Lucky was exasperated. 'You're hopeless.' She looked at Oliver, who wasn't wet, but who *was* laughing. 'And you, too.'

'Am not,' Oliver said, then stuck out his tongue.

Lucky wished Aunt Cora had seen that! Maybe then she'd realise the truth about Julian and Oliver.

'Forget about them,' Pru said, pulling back Lucky. 'Let's get the horses painted up – even a little bit of colour would be good – and start the activities. We're running out of time.'

Lucky huffed. 'Fine.' She gave a deep stare at her cousins. 'But don't interfere. I promised you could take the kids this afternoon, but the deal is off if you mess with our plans again.' She turned to Oliver. 'And until lunch, you're still my kid.' She reached out her hand. 'You will participate, and you will like it.'

'I promise I won't like it,' Oliver said, but he still took her hand.

'We'll see.' Lucky whistled for Spirit. He came running and followed her into the riding ring.

Diary Entry

I knew that one hour of O-Mok-See wasn't going to be enough. There were just so many amazing things that we could do, like riding and games and snacks ... It was frustrating to try to fit in everything we'd planned. We had narrowed the activities down to thirteen great ideas, but had to focus on just a few, because the kids lost time making new warrior designs on the horses. Pru and Abigail and I decided we'd ride along, but wouldn't be timed. This event was for the kids.

First up, there was an individual time trial in barrel racing. While I helped the kids saddle up, Pru and Abigail rushed to roll out three barrels in this pattern:

The horses had to gallop around the empty wooden rain barrels in a cloverleaf pattern.

Everyone loved it. Especially Lester, who was surprisingly fast on a gentle little horse named Malu. He flew around those barrels and beat even Turo, who'd had the fastest barrel time in town until then.

Next up, we moved those light barrels into a straight row and everyone got an egg in a spoon. They rode the horses as fast as they could, weaving between the barrels. There'd be prizes for the quickest and then prizes for bravely trying, in case someone (like Stella) wanted to go real slow.

Lilly had a good start until her egg fell and shattered in the dirt. Snips won the timed event. That was, right up until Abigail discovered that he had cheated. Snips had put a drop of honey in the spoon to 'glue' down the egg. We never would've known, except the blue ribbon for the event stuck to his hand! Stella, to our surprise, had the second-best time, so she won the spoon game. She isn't so scared anymore ... and that girl has such a brave streak, I never would have guessed!

As we set up for the boot relay, Oliver declared that he wasn't participating. There was nothing I could do. Not as if I could throw him on a horse.

He announced that he was interested in riding only Spirit and no other horse. But that isn't how Spirit works. I tried to explain that to him. Spirit does what Spirit wants. And I'm the only one who rides him. I told Oliver that he could pick another horse, but he refused and sat back down under that tree, where he'd been sitting every day since the beginning of the club.

Still, for a guy who was protesting everything, I did catch him glancing up to see what was going on. That was encouraging.

'Okay, everyone.' Pru began explaining the boot relay. 'Stay on your horse, but slip off your boots and give them to a counsellor. We'll put them all in this wheelbarrow.' She pointed at the red wagon. 'Abigail will take them to the end of the arena and dump them in a big pile.'

The kids quickly shed their shoes as we divided them into teams.

'You sure you don't want to be on a team?' I asked Oliver as a last try before the O-Mok-See had to end.

He looked up at me sitting on Spirit, and shrugged.

So much for my thinking he might be softening.

'That's not happening,' I said and Spirit whinnied.

'Fine, then!' Oliver said in a big dramatic huff. 'I'll go make my own fun. I don't need you.'

The frustration I had with him bubbled up. 'Fine,' I countered. 'Just sit here, and soon you can go with Julian to do some dangerous thing.' I said, sneering 'Try not to get hurt.' He was so stubborn and I'd lost my patience. If he wanted to grow up to be just like his con man brother, then he should do that! I wouldn't try to stop him.

I turned Spirit around and we went back to the group.

'Ride on down to the far end of the arena. One at a time, riders from each team will gallop to the boots.' Abigail had spilled their boots and mixed them up in a pile. She was reading off the final rules now. 'Jump off your horse, find your own boots, put them on, get back on the horse and hurry back to your group.'

With a disappointed look at Oliver, I finished it up: 'When you reach the group, the next rider goes. The first team to get boots on all the riders wins the day.'

'We're riding horses without shoes?' Stella glanced down at her fancy riding boots, which she had so far refused to take off. They looked as if they were polished each night after the club. 'I'm not wearing socks.'

I shrugged. 'You can skip this one.' I didn't like how I talked to Stella. I was just so frustrated with Oliver!

'I want to ride twice. I'll go once for me and once for Stella,' Snips offered. 'I can take my boots back to the other end of the ring and go again.'

'I guess,' Stella said. She seemed uncomfortable with sitting out, but she didn't want to be barefoot in the horse ring, either.

'Okay, Snips goes twice,' Abigail said, leading Boomerang to the spot where the boots would go. 'Let's start this Boot Scoot Relay!'

'That's so cute,' Pru said. 'Who called it a "Boot Scoot"?'

Abigail smiled. 'I just made that up.'

When Pru and I went to help the kids pile their boots, she told me, 'You gotta stop worrying about Oliver.'

'I'm trying,' I replied. 'It's hard not to worry.' My anger at him for not even trying was mixed with disappointment that I couldn't convince him to give the O-Mok-See a go.

Pru nodded.

Abigail called everyone to the side of the ring. She was helping Snips pull off his boots, when she yanked so hard she tumbled backward.

'Hey! If Stella wants some socks so she can ride,' Abigail reported, looking at Snips's feet, 'I think Snips is wearing at least five pairs.'

'I like them stacked for warmth,' Snips replied, even though it was a hot day.

'I'm not wearing his socks.' Stella plugged her nose.

'I will!' Bianca cried.

'<u>Eww!</u>' Snips was horrified at the thought of giving up one of his many socks.

The shoes were in the pile.

At the last minute, Stella decided to ride. She announced that she'd wash her feet twice later.

The groups were divided into boys versus girls:

Turo, Snips and Lester versus Bianca, Mary Pat, Stella and Lilly.

Since Oliver was out, the teams were uneven, but at least Snips got to go twice.

I approached Oliver. 'Are you sure you don't want to join the boys' team?' I felt as if I'd make one last try to get him to play. I was even close to seeing whether he could ride Spirit, but when I reached towards Spirit, he reminded me with a huff that he called the shots.

Oliver huffed, too, and turned away.

The horses and their riders were ready at one side of the ring. The boots were waiting at the other.

'Riders, take your mark,' Pru called out. '<u>GO!</u>'

It was Snips versus Mary Pat. She grabbed her boots and slipped them on easily while Snips was struggling to pull his over all his socks. By the time he got back on Señor Carrots, Mary Pat had already tagged her sister.

'Like the wind,' Snips told Señor Carrots, who is surprisingly fast for a donkey.

Turo picked up speed against Bianca, and the two of them were neck and neck, when ...

'Time's up! It's noon!' Julian was hanging by the gate to the riding ring.

He leaned a shovel against the fence and dropped his canvas pack.

Turo yanked so hard on the reins of his horse, Junipero, that the stallion nearly threw him off. Bianca took advantage of the confusion by jumping off her horse and running for the boots.

Julian stopped her. 'Hey, little lady, it's time to go on a real adventure,' he said. 'Enough of this boring horse stuff.'

I was surprised at the kids' reactions.

'It's not boring!' Bianca said.

Mary Pat echoed her. 'We're having lots of fun.'

Snips told Julian that he was messing up the competition and that he'd better get out of the way.

I will admit: I was proud of the kids. They were holding their ground.

'There are other team competitions we can do,' I told them, giving a side-eye to Julian. The mood had shifted and I was feeling pretty good.

I rattled off a few more games, like flag tipping and a game in which teams have to ride fast while tossing balls in a bucket.

'Ooohh,' Snips said. 'Bucket ball...'

Julian raised his shovel. 'But I'm taking everyone to Dusty Dan's grave. Let's eat lunch fast now, because we're going to dig for treasure. Everyone loves searching for treasure, right?' He looked around. No one argued.

'Especially when Julian gets the rewards,' I muttered. Then, as Pru and

Abigail came to stand with me, I said out loud, 'Let's make this fair. You should go on the treasure hunt if you want, but don't forget what happened last time.'

When they got back, we'd have our vote.

I could see the kids struggling with the decision to leave the barn.

Finally, I encouraged them to stay, asking, 'Who wants to find out who wins the Boot Scoot?'

A cheer went up from every single one of the kids.

Stella wiggled her toes in the dirt. 'I'd like to get my boots,' she said. 'And win for my team!'

'Now, who wants to go on a real adventure?' Julian asked.

No one replied to Julian's question, so he asked it again.

'Maybe you didn't hear me: Who wants to go on an adventure?'

Julian's booming question was met by uncomfortable silence.

There wasn't even a peep from the one kid I expected to eagerly whoop and holler.

I turned around. There was no one under the tree.

I asked Julian what happened to Oliver.

He answered slowly, scanning the horizon. 'I don't know.'

Julian's pack and shovel were still sitting by the fence.

Oliver was missing.

CHAPTER 6

'What are we going to do?' Abigail, Pru and Lucky were meeting while Julian rushed around the barn, calling Oliver's name.

'I don't think he's in the barn,' Pru said, piecing her thoughts together. 'I'm starting to think Oliver's just been *pretending* he wanted to ride Spirit, knowing no one can ride him except Lucky. In fact, I think he's afraid of horses! I bet he threw that apple so he wouldn't have to hand it to the horses like Stella did!' She put her hand on her head as it all became perfectly clear. 'That's why he sat under the tree, even after the jig was up with

Julian. He wouldn't participate in the O-Mok-See because he was scared!'

Lucky considered that. Certainly he hadn't ridden another horse, but was he scared? She had seen him interact with the horses only once. 'He washed the horses with Julian.'

'With *Julian*,' Pru repeated. 'But he didn't get wet. I don't think he helped much at all.' Lucky nodded. She'd noticed that Oliver's shirt was completely dry while Julian's was wet. Pru went on: 'That kid wants so desperately to be like his brother, if Julian said 'go swim in the creek,' he'd try to turn into a fish.'

Lucky sighed. 'I guess I never really had a shot at changing him, did I?'

Pru shook her head with a supportive look. 'Nope. But I didn't want to ruin your dreams.'

Abigail was catching on. 'If he wants so desperately to be like Julian, do you think he went to Dusty Dan's grave site on his own? To try to impress him?'

'I think we should check it out,' Lucky said. 'The other kids didn't want to go with Julian, so maybe Oliver wanted to prove to Julian that he was still his biggest fan.' Lucky whistled for Spirit. 'Abigail, you're a genius!'

'Uh, hello ...' Pru pointed to herself.

'Also a genius,' Lucky agreed. Spirit was ready to go to Dusty Dan's grave site, when Julian came out of the barn, leading Malu.

'We have to go to Dusty Dan's,' he said, preparing to climb into the saddle.

'Dusty Dan?' Snips stuck his head into the conversation. 'But we agreed to finish the O-Mok-See.' He whined. 'We voted.'

'Democracy is a complicated work in progress,' Stella moaned. 'It's a sad day when voting doesn't mean anything.'

Lucky climbed onto Spirit. 'Abigail and Pru

can continue with the O-Mok-See,' she told the kids. 'Julian and I will search for Oliver.' She looked out in the direction he would have gone. 'He can't be that far on foot.'

'We aren't staying back,' Pru said, with a determined expression. 'You might need us and I doubt that city-boy Julian is the handiest on horseback.' Pru paused and turned to speak to the kids. 'Listen up! Looks like we're all going on a treasure hunt after all. There's only one thing on the list: Oliver! He's – *uhh* – hiding, so we can find him!'

'Let's go find my friend Ollie!' Snips cheered. 'Tomorrow, he'll be on our team and we will beat you all!'

'Except that Ollie doesn't ride,' Pru whispered to Lucky.

She thought about that. 'Maybe ... we'll see ...'

'See what?' Pru asked, but Lucky was already busy getting the kids on their horses.

There was a mighty cheer from the kids, and they began to chant, 'Ollie! Ollie! Ollie!'

As soon as everyone was ready, Lucky and Spirit led the way from the stables toward the path to Dusty Dan's. 'Yee-haw!' She pressed into Spirit's flank and he began to gallop.

Julian pulled up beside her. 'A treasure hunt, eh?'

'You were the one who convinced Oliver they were boring,' Lucky said.

'I see that might not have been the best idea,' Julian said. He was hiding it, but Lucky could clearly tell that losing Oliver had shaken him up. 'I wish I'd encouraged him to look for horse bridles and pinecones,' Julian admitted. 'Then we wouldn't be in this mess.' He bit his lip. 'What are we going to do?'

'*We'll* find Oliver,' she said, 'then *you'll* do

your best to convince him that PALs Club is plenty exciting.'

Julian agreed, nodding.

She pressed Spirit even faster, ready to make the turn for the creek, when Pru called out, 'Lucky! You're going the wrong way!'

'Dan's grave is over here,' she called back, sensing Chica Linda slowing behind them.

Pru had not only changed directions; she was leading the kids on a new path – away from Dusty Dan's grave!

Lucky and Spirit swung around. Julian and Abigail followed.

'What's going on?' Lucky asked Pru when she caught up. 'Why'd you stop?'

'Oliver wasn't going to Dusty Dan's,' Pru answered, climbing down from Chica Linda.

'You can't stop now,' Julian told her. 'Get back on the horse. Oliver needs me.' He corrected, 'I mean, he needs *us*.'

Pru had more experience in tracking than the others. She ignored him and said, 'We need to go on more than a hunch.' Taking a handful of dirt, she let the sand sift through her fingers. 'Oliver didn't go to Dan's grave.'

'Of course he did,' Julian countered. 'He wanted treasure.'

Lucky realised something then. 'If he wanted the treasure, he'd have taken the shovel to dig. I saw it before we left! It was still by the fence.'

'He also didn't know the way and wouldn't be able to get there without Julian guiding,' Pru went on.

Abigail looked at Julian and asked, 'You didn't take him there before today, did you?'

'No,' Julian admitted.

'Okay, kids,' Lucky announced. 'Who has an idea how to find Ollie?'

Diary Entry

This is not going to be easy.
<u>Think, Lucky, think!</u>

<u>I'm writing down all the kids'</u>
<u>clues.</u>

Lilly: 'Oliver went somewhere he
knew.'

Lester: 'Somewhere dangerous.'

Snips: 'Somewhere fun and exciting.'

They were all solving the mystery
together.

<u>We finally put it together. Oliver is</u>
<u>at the rocky outcrop.</u>

<u>This is not good.</u>

<u>That place is actually dangerous.</u>

CHAPTER 7

Pru found shoe prints in the dirt.
Lucky had hoped to catch her young
cousin along the path, but by the time they
got to the place where the footprints faded
into the first ridge of boulders, Oliver was
nowhere in sight.

The kids all scanned the higher rocks,
while Lucky warned them, 'Be careful. Those
rocks can slip and cause an avalanche.' As
she said it, two small stones came tumbling
down from a place high on the ridge.

'There!' Julian called out. 'I see him.' His
brother was a speck clinging to a high rock.
The top of the outcrop loomed high above

him. He'd made it about halfway up the large pile of stones. 'Oliver!'

'Ollie!' Snips called.

'Oliver ... Ollie ...' the hills echoed.

Lucky sprang forward with Spirit, but each step that Spirit made dislodged more stones.

'Stop,' Pru ordered.

'We'll get crushed if you go up that way,' Abigail said, pushing the kids back a safe distance.

Julian dismounted from Malu and started on foot up the way Oliver had gone. He also sent rocks falling with every step.

'You can't go that way,' Lucky told him, pulling Spirit back to the bottom of the hill.

Suddenly, Oliver's voice echoed down the hillside. 'Help! Julian! Help!'

He'd seen them all below.

And from where they were, they all could

151

see him, too. Feet dangling, Oliver was
clinging to a large, ragged rock. Several
medium-size stones rolled down from
where he was, and the group had to move
back farther to avoid being hit as the rocks
tumbled fast and crashed into the brush.

'Oliver!' Julian cried.

Oliver managed to swing himself to a safe
place, but he was clutching the boulder like
a spider, unable either to climb farther up or
slide back down.

'This is all my fault,' Julian said, starting
forward again. 'I'll go up there and get him.'

'No you won't,' Lucky said. 'You'll start an
avalanche and we'll *all* be in danger.'

She gathered with Pru and Abigail. 'What
do we do?'

'There's a horse path to the top,' Abigail
said. 'It's pretty safe that way, but we need to

lead the horses carefully. If they knock one stone, it might hit another and another and ... *kaboom!*' She used her hands to show the damage an avalanche would cause. Booming, like an explosion.

'We don't want a kaboom,' Julian said, joining them.

'So here's what we'll do.' Lucky spelled it out. 'Pru, Abigail and I are going to ride up the ridge and rescue Oliver.'

'I'm going, too,' Julian insisted.

'Nope.' Pru put up a hand. 'To avoid a kaboom, we need the most experienced riders on this. That's not you.' She eyed the kids. 'Someone has to keep the kids safe.'

'Oh, the irony,' Abigail said. 'The guy who wanted to lead them into danger now has to protect them.' She looked to her friends. 'Do we trust him?'

153

Another small rock slide scattered down the hills from above them and they all heard Oliver grunt.

'He can't hold on long,' Lucky told Julian. 'Do you agree to stay with the kids or not?'

He didn't hesitate. 'I'll stay.'

'If even one of them gets a pebble in their shoe,' Lucky said, 'I'm telling Aunt Cora everything.'

Julian frowned. 'I'll stay. Don't worry. I'll entertain them.' He moved Malu back to be with the kids. 'Who wants to hear a story about my greatest adventures? I've been on so many ... Where to even start?'

Lucky nodded at Pru and Abigail. 'I hope he has a lot of interesting stories,' she said.

'We'd better hurry,' Abigail said.

Chica Linda, Boomerang and Spirit took

154

off toward the small path that wove around to the top of the outcrop.

'Oliver, hang on,' Lucky shouted as the horses neared the top edge of the canyon. The slightest misstep would cause rocks to fall from the top, raining down onto Oliver's head. If he let go, he'd be swept into an avalanche of heavy stones.

'I can't wait much longer,' Oliver whined, his voice echoing against the rocks. 'My hands are slipping.'

'We have to work fast,' Pru told Abigail as she unwound a thick rope from Chica Linda's saddle. Abigail took the end of the rope and tied it around her waist, then handed the loose end to Lucky.

'I'll stay here and hold on like an anchor,' Abigail said, wrapping her arms around the nearest tree. 'You get the rope to Oliver and he can pull himself up.'

Lucky liked that idea. She tied the loose end of the rope around her own waist. 'Okay, I'm going down to get him,' she said.

'Wait, I meant I could pull up only Oliver. I don't think I can hold the two of you,' Abigail said, moving away from the tree. 'Oliver is little. No offense, Lucky, but him *plus* you equals more than *me*.'

'I can hold you back,' Pru suggested, wrapping her arms around Abigail's waist, and then the two of them held the tree. Even so, the unstable ground was brittle under their feet. One slip could send Lucky and Oliver *and* Abigail and Pru down to the canyon floor far below!

They came up with a third plan, which was to wrap the rope around the steady tree. That worked even better.

Lucky smiled at her friends and said, 'I'll be right back.' She carefully moved to the edge of the path. A small pebble skidded from under her foot and bounced its way down the rocks, narrowly missing Oliver's right hand.

'Oliver,' Lucky said, 'I'm coming down. Do not move.'

'I'm not moving,' he promised. 'But hurry. My hands are very slippery.'

Lucky stepped down onto a boulder, testing the stability before putting all her weight down. Pru and Abigail held the rope tight around the tree.

She moved down another stone, and a few more, until there were about ten big stones between her and Oliver.

To keep him focused, Lucky counted them as she moved, slowly, methodically testing each rock before setting her feet firmly on it. 'Three. Four. Five. Hang on, Oliver ...'

'I don't think I can much longer, Lucky,' Oliver said. 'My hands really hurt.'

'Six,' Lucky said. 'Don't think about it. That's seven. I'm almost there.'

'I can't—'

'Want to hear the story of how I learned to ride Spirit?' Lucky suggested. She stepped to a rock just to the side of where Oliver was still hanging on for his life. 'See, it started when my dad learned he was needed in Miradero ...'

As she lowered herself onto the rock next to him, which would have brought her side by side, the big stone creaked and began to slide out from under her feet. Lucky shouted to Pru and Abigail. 'Hold the rope!' They pulled the rope firm and held her until she could find another place to steady her weight.

Then Lucky cried out to Julian below, 'Move the kids back!' She couldn't look to see whether he'd done it.

That one rock hit the one below it and on

and on until a rock slide formed. Lucky knew this was going to be bad. 'Oliver,' she said, 'grab my hand.' She reached out her palm toward him while rocks banged and crashed below them.

Oliver screamed. 'I'm scared.'

Lucky looked him in the eye and said, 'Me too.' She stretched her hand even closer to him.

Oliver reached out so he was clinging to the boulder with only one hand. 'I can't stay … Lucky …' Oliver shrieked as his other hand slipped and he began to fall.

Lucky swung herself forward and grabbed Oliver around the waist. She held him tight. They were both hanging off the side of the rocks. 'Pull us up!' Lucky called to her friends.

'Uh, problem,' Abigail replied. Suddenly, it felt as if the rope had been loosed and they were going to plummet to the ground below, but an instant later, the rope went taut.

'Problem solved.' Abigail stuck her head over the edge and gave a small thumbs-up.

'Who's holding the rope?' Lucky asked, trying desperately to hang on to Oliver.

There was a loud sound of hooves and suddenly Lucky and Oliver began to rise toward the top of the outcrop, where the path was sturdy.

'Spirit,' Lucky breathed. Of course, it was Spirit!

Small pebbles fell forward, but Spirit continued to pull.

Oliver closed his eyes and put his head against Lucky's neck.

She continued to hold tight to him as they rose slowly toward the top.

One last tug and they made it over the top onto solid land.

Lucky looked around. The tree where Pru and Abigail had tied the rope had uprooted and tipped over. That was why the rope hadn't held. Spirit had saved them both.

'I'm so glad you're safe,' Pru said, dashing forward to hug Lucky. She looked at Oliver and frowned. 'Oliver, how could you be so reckless?'

Lucky put out a hand to help him up. 'He just wanted some adventure ... and to be like Julian.'

'But he almost got you both killed!' Pru protested.

Oliver rose, dusted himself off, and faced Pru, Abigail and Lucky. 'I'm sorry, Lucky. I was mixed up,' he said. 'I didn't mean to get anyone hurt.'

Lucky squeezed his shoulder. 'I know you didn't, Oliver.'

'Maybe all adventures don't have to be dangerous like Julian said. Maybe ... maybe we can have adventures like you and Pru

and Abigail do. Can I come back to PALs
Adventure Club?'

'You know what, Oliver?' Lucky asked
with a small chuckle, 'I think that sounds
great, too.'

Diary Entry

It's been a wild summer in Miradero!
I can hardly believe that today is the
final day of the O-Mok-See!

All of Miradero is invited
to participate.

There are horse games and prizes.
We're even running competitions that
Boomerang, Chica Linda and Spirit could
compete in. In fact, I'm writing
this during the break before one that
Spirit and I are running in right now!

Mr Winthrop brought a wagon loaded
with ice cream for everyone and Abigail
made cherry pies. Aunt Cora brought

more of her cookies. Dad and Kate are here, too.

While the kids decorated their horses and got into costumes for the day, Pru, Abigail and I met near the barn.

Club wasn't over yet and after the start of the O-Mok-See, there were new kids who wanted to sign up. New kids means more money. We've been working hard and earning it! In the end, there'd been enough to buy Aunt Cora the bubble bath and some new decorations for the barn, too.

This turned out to be the best summer after all.

Then, it was time for the Boot Scoot. That's everyone's favourite game and we'd started to do it every day. Today, the teams were mixed. Lester and Lilly with Stella and Turo versus Snips and Bianca and Mary Pat and Oliver!

Pru was right: Oliver <u>had</u> been afraid to ride, so I'd been taking him out after the club, teaching him the basics and now he was ready. He rode Malu, who's the most gentle of the barn horses.

Just before the Boot Scoot began, Julian came to me. He held his hands behind his back.

'I got something,' he said, bringing his hands around and opening his palms.

Rainbows from the small crystal bottle glittered in the sunlight.

'You bought it?!' I was immediately mad. 'I have the money! You can't give

it to your mum. Please! I need that for
Aunt Cora—'

'Slow down, RF,' Julian said. 'I got
it for you.' He handed me the crystal.
It was filled with the lavender bubble
bath that Cora loved. 'It's a thank-you
present for saving Oliver. Now you can
keep all the money you earned.' He gave
a suave smile. 'Buy yourself something
you want.'

'I don't know what I want ...'

I considered it. I never expected to have
this much extra money all to myself.

'Then give me the money,' Julian
joked. 'And I'll buy something I want.'

I shoved my money into my pocket. 'I'll
think of something,' I assured him.

'I better go,' he said, looking over
his shoulder.

Aunt Cora found out that Julian had put Oliver in the club, when he was supposed to be watching him. She dragged him to town, and now he works my old job at the ice cream shop. I'm not sure how Cora convinced Mr Winthrop that he did need help after all, but I smiled as Julian slipped my old frilly apron over his head and stepped behind the wagon cart to sell ice cream at the O-Mok-See.

Then Spirit came to get me and together we strode tall and proud into the ring, ready to start the O-Mok-See in front of the whole town.

I gotta go, though, Diary. Now that the kids have finished their Boot Scoot, it's the counsellors' turn. Me versus Pru versus Abigail – may the best PAL win!

Join Pru on the next adventure!

Kirkus calls **DreamWorks**
Spirit Riding Free: The Adventure Begins,

'A wild ride that will make spirits soar.'